THE STORY OF
JESUS

tales from the New Testament
retold for children

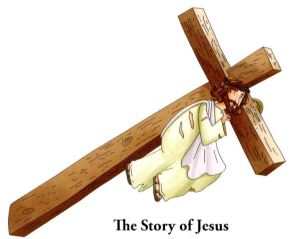

The Story of Jesus
© 2022 North Parade Publishing,
Written by Janice Emmerson
Illustrations by QBS Learning

Published by North Parade Publishing, Bath BA1 1LF, United Kingdom

Printed in China

Contents

The Birth of Jesus

Mary lived in the village of Nazareth. She was happy and excited, for she was engaged to be married to Joseph, a local carpenter.

One day, an angel of God appeared before her. He said gently, "Don't be afraid, Mary. God has chosen you for a special honour. You will give birth to a baby boy, and you are to call him Jesus. He will be called the Son of God, and his kingdom will never end!"

Mary was filled with wonder. "How can this be?" she asked softly.

"Nothing is impossible for God," replied the angel. "The Holy Spirit will come on you, and your child will be God's own Son."

Mary trusted God with all her heart. "I am God's servant," she said. "I'll do whatever God wants me to."

4

God spoke to Joseph in a dream and explained everything. Joseph married Mary straight away and took good care of her.

But soon they had to travel to Bethlehem. You see, at exactly this time, the Emperor of Rome decided to order a census. The Emperor was a very powerful man and he ruled over many, many lands. He wanted to keep track of every single person in all the lands that he ruled over. He wanted to make sure that everyone paid their taxes! And so all the people throughout the lands ruled by Rome had to go to their hometown to be counted.

It so happened that Joseph's family was descended from King David, and so he and Mary had to travel to Bethlehem, where King David had been born. Mary's baby was due to be born any day, and the journey was long and hard, but, like everyone else, they had to
do as the Emperor ordered.

5

When Mary and Joseph finally arrived in Bethlehem, they were tired and desperately wanted to find a room for the night, for the time had come for Mary's baby to be born.

But the town was filled to bursting, for everyone had come to be counted. The houses were crowded as families squeezed in, and as for the inns, well, every single room in every single inn was full. By the time that Joseph and Mary arrived in Bethlehem, there was nowhere for them to stay!

Things seemed very bleak, but at last, one kind innkeeper took pity on them.

"I'm afraid I have no rooms free, but I do have somewhere you can spend the night," he said, and he showed them to a stable where the animals were kept. It was dirty and smelly, but at least they had a roof over their heads.

That night, Mary's baby was born. She wrapped him in strips of cloth, then laid him gently on clean straw in a manger—one of the troughs that the animals used for feeding. Mary and Joseph looked down upon their son with joy, and they named him Jesus, just as the angel had told them to.

And so, one of the prophesies of the Old Testament was fulfilled, for over seven hundred years before this, the prophet Isaiah had foretold that one day God would send a sign: "A young virgin will fall pregnant and will give birth to a son and will call him Immanuel."

You see, Immanuel means 'God is with us', and that is exactly what had happened—God had come to live with us on earth.
Jesus was Immanuel!

The First Visitors

That same night, on a hillside overlooking Bethlehem, some shepherds were watching over their sheep. All of a sudden, the dark night sky was ablaze with light, and the shepherds fell to the ground in fright as an angel of the Lord appeared in the sky above them.

"Don't be afraid," the angel said to them gently. "I'm here to bring you good news—the best! Today a very special baby has been born in King David's town—he is Christ, the Messiah, God's own Son! Go and see for yourselves. You'll find him lying in a manger in a stable."

8

Then the sky was filled with more angels, all singing a beautiful song praising God: "Glory to God in the highest heaven, and peace on earth and good will to all men!" And then, as swiftly as they had come, the angels disappeared.

In the silence that followed, the shepherds looked at one another in amazement. Had that really just happened? Had a host of shining angels just appeared to them, a bunch of dirty, raggedy shepherds?

But they didn't waste much time thinking about 'why?' for they were far too busy racing down to the town and searching for the stable where they would find the special baby. And when they did find Mary and Joseph, and little Jesus lying in the manger just as they had been told, their hearts exploded with joy and gratitude, and they rushed off to tell everyone they could find the amazing news.

9

In a distant land, three wise men studying the stars discovered a bright new star shining in the skies. They knew it was a sign that a great king had been born—and so they set off and followed the star all the way to Jerusalem.

They went first to the court of Herod the Great, to ask if he could show them the way to the baby who would be the king of the Jews.

Herod was horrified! He didn't want another king around! His advisors told him of a prophecy that the new king would be born in the city of King David, in Bethlehem, so the cunning king sent the wise men to Bethlehem, saying, "Once you've found him, come back and tell me where he is so I can visit him too!" He didn't say what sort of visit he wanted to pay him!

The wise men followed the star. They found Jesus and his parents in a humble house. Though he was only a child, they knelt before him, and presented him with gifts of gold, sweet-smelling frankincense, and myrrh before returning home. But they did not stop off at Herod's palace, for God had warned them in a dream not to go there.

When Herod realised they weren't coming back, he was furious. He was so angry he gave an order that every boy under the age of two in Bethlehem should be killed. He wasn't taking any chances!

But an angel appeared to Joseph in a dream, warning him to take his family to Egypt to keep them safe. He and Mary swiftly gathered their belongings, lifted little Jesus gently from his sleep, and set off in haste on the long journey to Egypt, where they lived until wicked King Herod died.

Then they returned to Nazareth, and as the years passed, Jesus grew to be filled with grace, wisdom and kindness.

Baptised in the River

Shortly before Jesus came into the world, another special baby was born. His name was John. He was Jesus' cousin, and God had a very special plan for him, for John was to prepare the way for Jesus.

When John grew up, he went to live in the desert. He spoke to any who would listen about God's plans, and he told them to repent and change their ways. Many truly were sorry, and if they were, John took them down to the River Jordan, and there he would baptise them in the water as a sign that all their sins had been washed away and that they could start a new life.

One day, John was amazed to see Jesus by the river. He knew exactly who he was! Which made him all the more shocked when Jesus asked John to baptise him!

"You can't be serious!" he protested. "I shouldn't be baptising you—I should be begging you to baptise me!"

But Jesus just smiled and told him that this was what God wanted, and so John took him into the river.

At the very moment that Jesus came up out of the water, the heavens opened and the skies shone brightly and, like a dove, the Holy Spirit rested on Jesus. Then a voice came from above, "This is my Son, and I love him. I am very pleased with him."

At last, the much longed-for King had come to save his people!

Tested in the Desert

It was nearly time for Jesus to start spreading God's message to his people, but first of all, there was something he had to do. The Holy Spirit led Jesus into the desert. For forty days Jesus stayed in the desert, and in all that time he ate no food.

Then the devil came to test him, saying, "If you're the Son of God, surely you can do anything. Just tell these stones to become bread."

Jesus answered calmly, "It says in the Scriptures, 'Man shall not live on bread alone, but on every word that comes from the mouth of God.' " He knew that food wasn't the most important thing in life.

Not to be put off, the devil took Jesus to the top of a temple and told him to throw himself off. "If you're the Son of God, surely his angels would rescue you?" he taunted.

But Jesus said, "It is also written: 'Do not put the Lord your God to the test.' "

The devil took Jesus to the very top of a high mountain and showed him the land that stretched for miles in every direction. "All you have to do is bow down and worship me, and I will give you all the kingdoms of the world!" he coaxed.

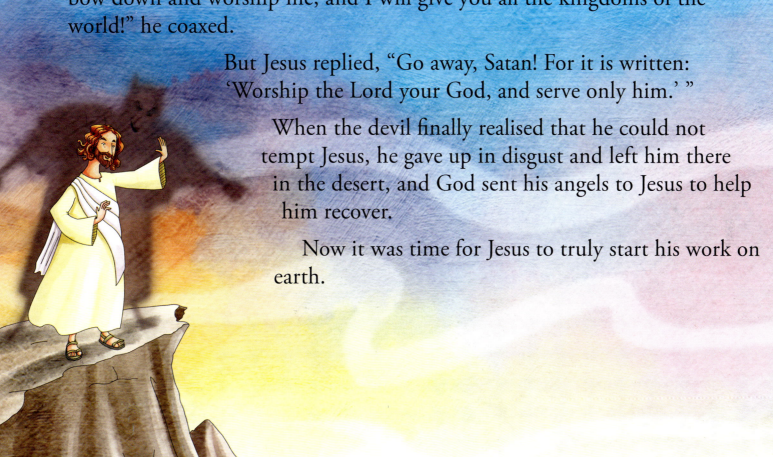

But Jesus replied, "Go away, Satan! For it is written: 'Worship the Lord your God, and serve only him.' "

When the devil finally realised that he could not tempt Jesus, he gave up in disgust and left him there in the desert, and God sent his angels to Jesus to help him recover.

Now it was time for Jesus to truly start his work on earth.

Fishing for Men

Word soon spread of Jesus of Nazareth. Wherever he went, people wanted to listen to him talk about God's love and forgiveness. One day when he was preaching, he asked Simon the fisherman to take him out on his boat, so that everyone could hear and see him.

Later, Jesus told Simon to let down his nets. Simon had been out all night, and hadn't caught a thing, but this time when he pulled up his nets they were full of fish! He called to his brother, Andrew, and to his friends James and John to help. Soon the boats were full of fish!

Simon fell to his knees, but Jesus smiled. "Don't be afraid, Simon. From now on you shall be called Peter (the Greek word for 'rock') for that is what you will be." He turned to all the men. "Leave your nets," he said, "and come with me and fish for men instead, so that we can spread the good news!"

The four men left everything behind, and followed Jesus without a backward glance!

These were the first special friends that Jesus called to help him in his work, but they weren't the last. Over time, Jesus chose twelve men to be his disciples, to pass on his message of good news, and to be there, after his death, to carry on his work. They weren't all fishermen —there was also a tax collector, Matthew, another Simon who was a patriot who wanted to fight the Romans, and six more men: Bartholomew, Thomas, James son of Alphaeus, Philip, Judas (or Thaddeus) son of James, and Judas Iscariot.

Jesus knew they would have a hard task ahead of them. He wanted them to teach the people that God's kingdom is near, and to heal people too. Later on, these men became known as apostles, or messengers, for they were chosen especially by Jesus to pass on his message of good news.

God's Doctor

Jesus travelled from place to place, preaching God's message, and healing and comforting those who were sick and in trouble. Once, when someone asked him why he spent so much time with outcasts and sinners he replied, "If you go to a doctor's surgery, you don't expect to see healthy people— it's people who are sick who need to see the doctor. I am God's doctor. I have come here to save those people who are sinners and who want to start afresh. Those who have done nothing wrong don't need me!"

His message was for everyone who had an open heart and a willingness to listen. He especially loved children, for they are good and innocent. He was always surrounded by children, and sometimes his disciples tried to shoo them away. They thought he had far more important things to do than be bothered by pesky little kids!

But Jesus had other ideas. "Don't ever stop little children from coming to me," he told them sternly. "The kingdom of heaven belongs to them and all those who are like them."

Jesus beckoned one of the little children to come to him and put his arm around him.

"You see," he said, turning to the disciples, "whoever welcomes this child in my name welcomes me, and whoever welcomes me welcomes the one who sent me. For it is the one who is least among you who is the greatest. To enter heaven, you must be like a little child!"

19

Wise Words

More and more people wanted to listen to this wonderful man—but the priests and teachers of the law weren't always pleased to have him around. They wanted people to listen to *them*, not *him!* All too often, Jesus wasn't made welcome in the synagogues, so he would teach his disciples and his followers outside in the open air. Jesus taught them about what was truly important in life and gave them comfort and advice on how to live their lives.

He told them that while it is important to obey God's laws, that isn't enough—we need to understand the meaning behind them. He spoke of true forgiveness, even towards our enemies, and told his listeners that they should try to set a good example to others —but that they shouldn't do good things just to impress other people. We don't need anyone else's praise—God can see inside our hearts and he knows the truth!

He offered comfort, saying that all those who lived a hard life would one day be happy in heaven, and he urged them to never give up, however hard things seemed. And most of all, he spoke of God's wonderful, unchanging love for each and every one of us!

On the Mountain Top

Jesus climbed up a mountain to pray, taking with him Peter, James and John. All of a sudden, as Jesus prayed, the disciples looked up to see him changed. Light shone from his face, and his clothes became dazzlingly white! As they watched in wonder, Moses, who had led his people out of Egypt, and Elijah, greatest of the prophets, were suddenly there, talking with Jesus! Then a bright cloud covered them, and a voice said, "This is my own dear Son, whom I love. Listen to what he has to say, for I am very pleased with him!"

The disciples fell to the ground, too frightened to raise their eyes. Jesus came over and touched them. "Don't be afraid," he said softly, and when they looked up, they saw no one there except Jesus.

When Jesus was on earth, there were lots of different ideas about who he really was. But from that moment on, Peter, James, and John had no doubt at all about who Jesus was. He was the Son of God. God had said it, and that was that.

Jesus Enters Jerusalem

Jerusalem was packed to bursting. It was the Passover festival, and everyone had gathered to celebrate. There was something else to celebrate too, for Jesus had come to Jerusalem. People had heard of the things he had said, and the miracles he had performed. Many saw Jesus as their true king, and wanted to give him a king's welcome.

When Jesus entered Jerusalem, he was riding a humble donkey, but that didn't stop the excitement. Some of the crowd threw their cloaks or large palm leaves on the dusty ground before him. They cried out, "Hosanna to the Son of David! Blessed is the king who comes in the name of the Lord— the King of Israel!"

They hoped Jesus would free them from the Romans. They didn't understand that his kingdom wasn't in this world but in heaven. Jesus knew that in a short time these people would turn against him. He was starting the final stage of his earthly life, and he knew exactly what was going to happen to him—and that it was the only way to save those he loved for all time.

The first thing Jesus did when he came into the city, was to visit the temple. He was shocked and angry—the beautiful temple was filled with greedy, cheating money changers and market traders. They had set up shop to make money out of the poor people who came to make sacrifices to God.

Jesus instantly threw them all out—his Father's house should be a place of peace and prayer, not a den of thieves! He chased out the traders, and he pushed over the tables of the money changers. Now the temple was a quiet place once more, where people could come to pray and to learn about God, and find comfort.

The priests were furious. Not only had they made money out of the traders, but now people were flocking to the temple to listen to Jesus and to come to *him* for healing, rather than to *them*. As far as they were concerned, Jesus was a trouble maker, and he had to go! They just had to work out how!

The priests were looking for a reason—and a way—to arrest Jesus, but he was usually surrounded by his followers. They needed help—and that help came from one of Jesus' own disciples!

Judas Iscariot was dishonest. He looked after the money for Jesus and the other disciples, but he kept some back for himself instead of giving it to those in need. In the end, his greed made him do a very bad thing. Judas went to the chief priests in secret and asked them how much they would give him if he delivered Jesus into their hands.

The priests knew that Judas was one of Jesus' closest, most trusted friends. They offered him thirty silver coins . . . and Judas accepted! As soon as he had left the temple, the priests rubbed their hands in glee. Now they had someone else to do their dirty work for them.

From then on, Judas was waiting for the opportunity to hand Jesus over.

The Last Supper

Jesus and the disciples had gathered to celebrate the Passover feast. Jesus left the table, wrapped a towel around his waist, then, kneeling on the floor, began to wash and dry the disciples' feet like a servant. The disciples were shocked. Simon Peter protested, "Lord, you mustn't wash my dirty feet!"

Jesus replied gently, "You don't understand what I'm doing, Peter, but soon you will. Unless you let me wash away the dirt, you won't really belong to me." Then Jesus washed the rest of the disciples' feet, one by one, until they were all clean.

When he finished, he said, "Do you understand what I was doing? You call me 'Lord' and 'Teacher,' and that is what I am—but I'm your servant too. The master isn't more important than the servant. I washed your feet, so you should wash one another's feet too."

Jesus had washed their feet like a servant, so they could learn to do the same for one another.

Jesus was sad and troubled. He knew he would soon have to leave his friends. "Soon, one of you will betray me," he said sorrowfully. The disciples looked at one another in shock. Who could he mean? Jesus said softly to Judas Iscariot, "Go and do what you have to do," and Judas left. But the others still didn't understand.

Now Jesus handed around some bread, saying, "This is my body, which will be broken." Next, he passed around a cup of wine, saying, "Drink this— it is my blood, which will take away sin." He wanted them to remember this time with him, and hoped they would one day understand what he was really telling them.

Then he said that he would soon be leaving them. Simon Peter begged to be allowed to follow him, but Jesus said gently, "And yet you will disown me three times before the cock crows!" Peter was horrified. He knew he would never do such a dreadful thing!

26

The Betrayal

Jesus went to a quiet garden on the hillside to pray, asking Peter, James and John to wait nearby while he went to talk to his Father. His heart was filled with sadness, and he cried out, "Oh, Father, is there any other way? Does it have to happen like this?" yet his very next words were, "But let it be not as I want, but as you want."

What was going to happen would be terrible, but Jesus had chosen freely to do it. He knew this was the only way to save God's children. He needed to take their sins upon himself, and he needed to take their punishment too. He would be their scapegoat, so they could be free from their sins, and free to be close to God again. But he knew it was going to be very hard.

The disciples dozed off. At last he awoke them to say, "The hour has come. Get up, for the one who betrayed me is here!"

At that moment a huge crowd of people burst into the garden with lanterns and swords and clubs. At the head of them all was Judas Iscariot. He had told the chief priests that he would kiss Jesus so that they would know whom to arrest, and as Judas approached him, Jesus said sadly, "Oh, Judas, would you betray the Son of Man with a kiss?"

Simon Peter was filled with anger, and struck out with his sword, cutting off the ear of the High Priest's servant. But Jesus calmed him, and healed the man's ear, saying "Don't you think my Father would send a host of angels to save me if I asked him to? This has to happen—how else can all the prophets said about me be fulfilled?"

Ge turned to the soldiers. "I'm the one you have come to find," he said quietly. "Let the others go. You had no need to come with swords and clubs."

The disciples were filled with despair. They could see that Jesus wasn't going to try to escape or fight, and as he let himself be arrested, they ran away in fear and went into hiding.

28

The guards led Jesus to the house of Caiaphas, the chief priest of the Jews. He was waiting for them, along with the other high priests. They needed to find a reason to order Jesus' execution, but they had a problem—they didn't have any evidence against him. To overcome this obstacle, they paid some people to come and tell lies about him. Unfortunately the 'witnesses' couldn't seem to agree on the same story.

Caiaphas decided that the easiest thing would be to get Jesus to commit blasphemy (blasphemy is speaking about God in a disrespectful way).

"So," he said to Jesus, "tell us, are you the Son of God?"

"You have said it yourself," Jesus answered. "And I will tell you this: you will see the Son of God sitting at the right hand of the Almighty God, riding on the clouds of heaven."

"Enough!" Caiaphas cried. "This man claims to be the Son of God. This is blasphemy—he must die!"

The Cock Crows

When the soldiers took Jesus to be questioned, Simon Peter followed them, and waited fearfully outside, along with the guards. A servant girl caught sight of Peter. "Weren't you with Jesus of Nazareth? I'm sure I saw you with him," she said.

"No, no! You've got the wrong man!" Peter hissed quietly, terrified of what might happen if they thought he was one of Jesus' disciples.

The girl shrugged, but when she walked back, she said to one of the guards, "Don't you think he looks like one of Jesus' followers?"

"I told you, I don't have anything to do with him!" babbled Peter, but now everyone was looking at him. "You must be one," said one of the guards. "I can tell from your accent you're from Galilee."

"I swear I've never even met him!" cried Peter, his heart racing.

Just then, a cock crowed. Peter remembered what Jesus had said earlier. He wept in dismay—how could he have betrayed Jesus! He felt as if his heart had broken in two.

Pilate Washes his Hands

"This man must die!" Caiaphas had said, but it wasn't as straight-forward as that. The Jews weren't allowed to execute anyone—they needed to persuade the Romans to do it! So they decided to tell the Romans that Jesus was calling himself 'King of the Jews'. If Jesus claimed to be a king, that was treason—and in Rome, death was the penalty for treason!

Jesus was taken before Pontius Pilate, the Roman governor. Pilate realised pretty quickly that Jesus wasn't a threat at all. The man was clearly innocent, but that wasn't what the crowd wanted to hear—and by now quite a crowd had gathered to hear Pilate's judgement. Those same people who had cheered as Jesus entered Jerusalem, had been fed lies by the priests and Pharisees and now wanted blood!

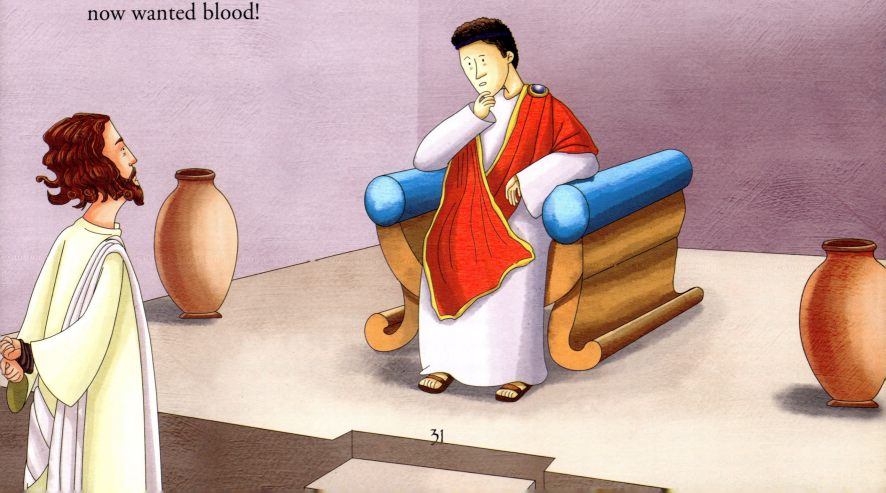

Pilate saw just one way out. It was Passover, and at Passover it was the custom to release one prisoner, so Pilate gave them two choices—Jesus of Nazareth (who had healed people and told stories about love and forgiveness) or Barabbas (in prison for rebellion and murder).

It should have been a fairly obvious choice. But the crowd had been whipped into a frenzy by the priests and Pharisees, and they all started chanting "Free Barabbas! Free Barabbas!"

"But what has Jesus done wrong?" asked Pilate, mystified.

In reply, the crowd shouted, "Crucify him! Crucify him!"

Pilate was dismayed, but he didn't want to start a riot. All he wanted was an easy life. So he called for a servant to bring him a bowl of water, and he washed his hands in it. "It's your call," he was saying to the people. "I had nothing to do with it!"

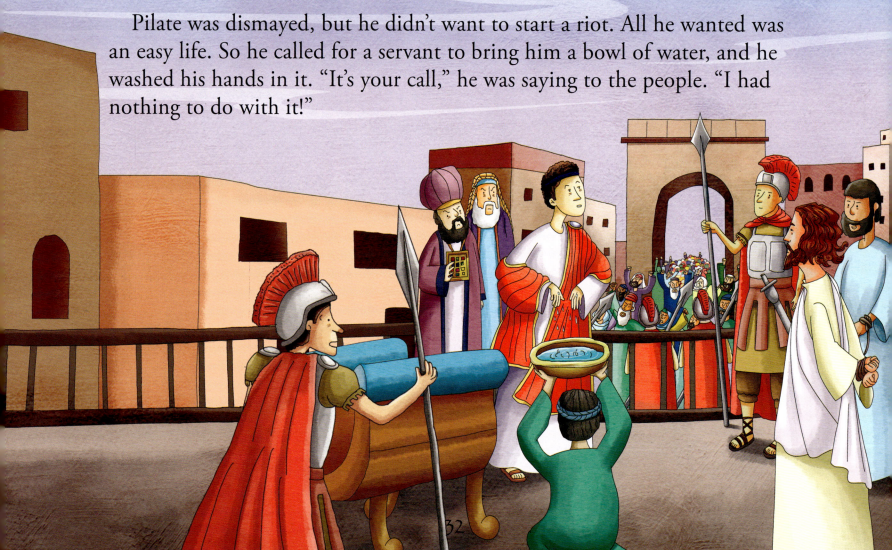

A Shadow Falls

Soldiers led Jesus away. "So you're King of the Jews, then?" they said mockingly. "Well then, let's make sure you look the part!" and they dressed him in a purple robe, the colour worn by kings, and put a crown of sharp thorny branches upon his head. Then they beat him, and spat in his face, before putting him back in his own clothes and leading him through the streets towards Golgotha, the place where he was to be crucified.

They made him carry the wooden cross on his back, but it was large and heavy, and Jesus had been dreadfully beaten and he had had no rest all night. When he could carry the cross no longer, they snatched someone from out of the crowd to carry it for him.

And so the dreadful procession made its way out of the city to the hill of Golgotha.

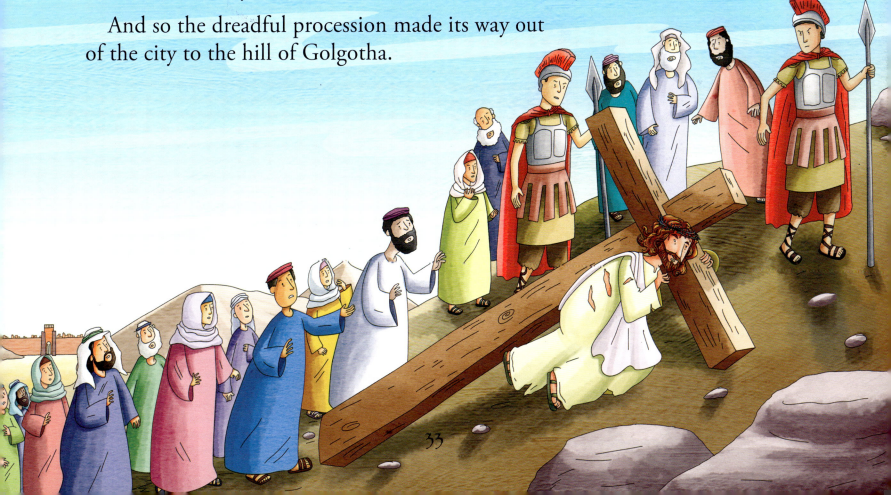

There on the hillside, soldiers nailed Jesus to the cross and placed above his head a sign saying, 'JESUS OF NAZARETH, KING OF THE JEWS'. As they raised the cross, Jesus cried, "Father, forgive them. They don't know what they're doing."

Two criminals were crucified beside him. "If you're so special why don't you save yourself? And me too, while you're at it!" one sneered.

But the other told him to be quiet. "We're here because we deserve to be," he said, "But Jesus has done nothing wrong." Then he asked Jesus, "Please remember me when you come into your kingdom," and Jesus promised he would be with him that very day in Paradise.

As Jesus hung there on the cross, down below the guards drew lots to see who would win his clothes, and the priests and Pharisees taunted him—"If you come down from the cross now, we'll believe in you!" they mocked.

Jesus could have chosen for all this to stop anytime he wanted. But he stayed there because he chose to—because he loved these people and wanted to save them from themselves.

At midday, a shadow passed across the sun, and dark clouds filled the sky. For three long hours darkness covered the land as though it were the middle of the night. At three o'clock in the afternoon, Jesus cried out in a loud voice, "My God, why have you forsaken me?" He bore the sins of all the people in the world, and so he felt all alone for the first and last time.

Then he let out a great cry—"It is finished!"—and with these words, he gave up his spirit and let himself die.

At that moment the earth shook, and in the city the curtain in the holy temple was torn from top to bottom, for Jesus, through his death, had removed the barriers between God and man. There is nothing now that comes between us and God.

Back on the hill, when the Roman soldiers felt the ground move beneath their feet and saw how Jesus passed away, they were deeply shaken. "Surely he was the Son of God!" whispered one in amazement.

The Empty Tomb

Though Jesus had always meant for this to happen, his friends were heartbroken at his death. They took his broken body down from the cross and carefully wrapped it, then took him to a tomb carved out of rock and laid his body inside.

But the priests and Pharisees remembered that Jesus had spoken of rising again, and so they asked Pilate to put guards on the tomb, and they had it sealed with a massive stone so that nobody could get in or out. That made sure none of his followers could pull some sort of clever stunt with his body to try to fool people!

"That's the end of Jesus!" said the chief priests smugly.

But, of course, they were wrong . . .

36

Three days later, early in the morning, Mary Magdalene and some other women went to anoint the body of their beloved teacher, hoping someone would move the heavy stone for them. As they came near, the earth shook, the guards were thrown to the ground, and the women saw that the stone had been rolled away from the entrance. Inside the tomb, shining brighter than the sun, was an angel!

The angel said to the terrified women, "Why are you looking here for someone who is alive? Jesus isn't here—he has risen! Didn't he tell you this would happen? Have a quick look, then tell his disciples he will meet them in Galilee just as he promised."

The women hurried away in excitement to tell the disciples the news, afraid yet filled with joy.

37

Later that day, Mary Magdalene stood weeping quietly outside the tomb. Some of the disciples had been to see, but now Mary was here by herself. Just then she heard the sound of footsteps behind her. A man asked gently, "Why are you crying? Who are you looking for?"

Thinking it was the gardener, she begged, "Sir, if you have moved him, please tell me where he is, and I'll get him."

The man only spoke her name, "Mary," but she recognised that clear, gentle voice! "Teacher!" she gasped. Was Jesus truly there? And she reached out towards him with her arms wide open.

Jesus said, "Dear Mary, you mustn't hold on to me, for I have not yet gone to my Father. Quick! Go and tell the others!" So Mary rushed off with the amazing news that she had seen Jesus alive!

Alive!

That same evening most of the disciples were together talking about the incredible events of the day, when suddenly Jesus was with them! He spoke with them and ate with them, and the men were filled with wonder and joy.

But Thomas wasn't there, and he didn't believe them. "Unless I see the holes with my own eyes, and put my finger where the nails were, I won't believe," he said angrily—because, of course, he *did* want to believe.

One week later, the disciples were all together, when Jesus appeared amongst them again. He turned to Thomas. "Do you believe now, Thomas?" he asked. "Come, look for yourself, touch the wounds with your own hands. Stop doubting, Thomas—and believe!"

"Oh, Lord, I *do* believe!" Thomas cried out, bursting with happiness.

Jesus smiled, "Thomas, you believed only because you saw me yourself, with your own eyes. Think about the people who believe without seeing. How blessed will they be!"

The Ascension

Jesus and his friends were on a hillside outside Jerusalem. It was time for him to leave the world. "Stay here and wait for the gift that my Father has promised you," he told them, "for soon you will be baptised with the Holy Spirit. Then you must spread my message not only here, but in every country throughout the world!"

Jesus held up his hands to bless them and then, before their eyes, he was taken up to heaven, and a cloud hid him from sight. Suddenly two men dressed in white stood beside them. "Why are you looking at the sky?" they asked. "Jesus has been taken from you into heaven, but he will come back again in the same way that he left!"

Jesus has gone to heaven to prepare a place for us, and one day he will come again to take us to our new home so that we can live forever in God's love.